Love; Trust;

Friendship;

&

Family

Love; Trust; Friendship; & Family

Four Most Commonly Misunderstood Words in the World Today

Glanda Woods

Printed in the United States of America

ISBN 978-1-257-83429-7

Table of Contents

Introduction

Ready for the truth, the whole truth, and nothing but the truth, then find the most comfortable seat wherever you are because you're about to go for a ride. The ride of this world, one that is smooth with no twists and turns but yet takes you through many deep valleys. These valleys surround you, me, and all that exist. Before takeoff, I would like for you to take a huge breath and exhale it out slowly just to prepare yourself for moments of silent thoughts you will encounter. Try to hold on to your seat. Like many others, I know you have seen, been through, and heard a lot, but I am going to share with you and everyone something many fail to realize. If you think you're ready then gear yourself into the drive position and slowly proceed to examine Love; Trust; Friendship; & Family: *Four Most Commonly Misunderstood Words in the World Today*. Feel free to go into reverse and backup as often as needed. Let's Go!

Love; Trust;

Friendship;

&

Family

Love

Looking around at things today you rarely see love in any form. Over the years, it has drastically diminished. Love use to be as one may call it the all-time-high. Back in the olden days, you saw it everywhere and among all things. It was not only there but glistened, showing its passion between people, places, and objects. You could look in ones face, eyes, or gesture and see loves radiance. Most of all it was simple. Love's a short, four letter, one syllable word that when spoken or expressed had such power, value, and meaning. What has happened to cause its disappearance? This question has left many people mine boggled,

Love; Trust; Friendship; & Family

including myself.

Love has had a journey of its own. Just like many of us love has been through the wringer and left hung out to dry. It has transformed into having multiple meanings, levels, types, and reasons. Love is known for causing many deeds both good and bad. Overtime it has done more damage than Hurricane Katrina and healing than antibiotics. Just like many medicines it has numerous side effects some worse than others. Just think of all the repercussions of love. Ever notice how one word triggers so many words:

- Happiness
- Births
- Marriage

Love

- Divorce
- Tears
- Sorrow
- Smiles
- Frowns
- Depressions
- Death
- Pain
- Illness
- Disturbance
- Mystery
- Passion
- Regret
- Sin
- Knowledge
- Anger
- Secrets
- Sex
- Confidence

- Trust
- Friendship
- Family

The list is extensive. Nor will you or I ever know its length. As always, love is unpredictable when found and ended. Its journey is often traveled only to find that love is lost and misunderstood.

Surely there are no limits to the repercussions of love. Therefore, the question to ask is. Why is love so limited? Of course, it causes heartache and pain but most aftermaths of love is much more glorious. The insight, gained wisdom, knowledge, peace of mind and soul, and most of all the purity of the heart to continue to love and find love in all things from love trials is priceless. Love should be thought of and savored more than money. One may endure money and think he has prospered but until one has love will he reach prosperity. You may enter the gates of Ford Field or Comerica Park with money, but you will need a heart of love to enter the pearly white gates.

As each decade or generation has changed so has love. Something pure has become more complex than ever. People simply have change to the point where they just don't love anymore. Nowadays, folks need a purpose to love. As humans and the children of the almighty we never needed a purpose for him to love us. So how do people dare change something as precious as love?

Many aim to love those connected to them. Presuming, as if they are the only ones in existence and others don't matter. Even those in conjunction aren't loved these days without a purpose. In the times that have come, we all know that purpose could be just about anything. Clearly, it is shown that one has to be beneficial to one or the other in order for some form of love to be of presence. The questionable saying, "what can you do for me?" has made its mark. It is so deeply expressed in the hearts and actions of people that the words itself need not to be spoken.

From time to time, you may see small notions of love, but even it can be easily wilted away. The strength of love has been devoured by all the worldly possessions that currently lurk among us. Out of the entire thing that pulls people apart it seems that only death has the power to resurface love again. It should not have to be this way but as truthful as it may be it is. From the very beginning love and death had a connection. Remember that the death of Jesus took place out of love for us. The difference from then and now is that love was first and ultimate.

Love is not exempt. It has not been taken away from us nor are we forbidden to love. The disappearance of it is solemnly on our own behalf. As humans, people of this world have literally thrown love under the bus. By doing so, they have practically turned their backs on our creator. Look at all the destruction and devastation that have been submerged from this. Is there any way to put ourselves in reverse and rescue love from its fatal fall? We need it to survive.

People in this world have been fighting for centuries. Fighting for all the things they saw fit to fight for. Some things were worthy and some weren't. The worthiest of them all is love and that battle must have been lost. I know that many of us are tired, but we have to continue to fight at least one last round. As with previous times various heroes put their hearts and lives on the line. Now we all must do so to bring love back. In this fight,

Love

God is the chief, commander, coach, and referee. We need not to skip a beat. There are no time outs and no room for retreats. This is supposed to be a land of love. It can be conquered if everyone starts shooting out caring souls filled with joyful laughs, big smiles, open arms, and gracious words.

Love is not a stranger to no one. It may sometimes seem as if though it is hidden, but it never is. Love has always sat in that same corner waiting to be tagged by its partner, you, me, her, him, or anyone. At different points in life people want to show off the things that they can do. They tend to have a lot of heart and think big of it. That is where boasting and bragging may come in. If someone truly has a big heart then why don't they place it center stage and step back to allow love to show its stuff and how things are really done. Now that's something to talk about or maybe even brag.

There is so much going on every day that has caused love to be forgotten. Everywhere you turn you hear about the fallen economy. How foreclosure is at its worst. The hard bang faced by the "Big Three" automakers and their comeback. The shortage of jobs in various areas that has affected people lives. There are many massive crimes being committed. Outrageous educational battles and downfalls have emerged. Let's not forget the weather's powerful onsets of storms, floods, tornados, and hurricanes. Believe it or not all these things at some interval have a lack of love in common. If we strived to regain love the same way we discuss, obsess, ponder on, oversee, and negotiate all these other dilemmas then maybe so much would not be lost including love.

We have constantly been told that nothing in this world is for free. I disagree with that. It does not cost anything to nod your head, put an arch in your cheeks and smile, say hello, or wave your hand to acknowledge someone. These actions play their role in showing love. Many things may carry a monetary value or have a series of cause and effect but love was given to us for free. Even though it cost our savior his life to love us, he didn't charge us anything. He only requested for us to live and characterize a list of good deeds. Then return to him with a blueprint of our deeds done. His list had love engraved on it so feel free to love. If you ever get billed for genuine love at any time, way, or form then sends the receipt to our father. He will surely open his wallet and pay your debt. The next thing you know whether it's now, or later you will receive a mail-in-rebate directly from him.

With the day to day changes, many people have forgotten how to love and some never knew how to at all. There is no science or strategy to it. Regardless of what the world imposes you can't really buy true love nor borrow it. Yes, it does require some common since, but most of all it requires you. If you're ready and willing to love again then take a look at yourself first. You can't give or show love to someone else until you find love for and within yourself. This does not mean to be selfish. It means to understand and be thankful for who you are, what you have or don't have, and where you're at in life despite any past or present difficulties. Try waking up every day with a graceful, peaceful, humble mine, body, and soul. Start recognizing troubled awkward areas and situations then separate you from them. Uses the will power handed down to you from our father and creates happiness. Ease up on the stress and worries and gain a more pleasant spirit. Keep a promising attitude by staying positive about all things not negative. Then last but not least have faith and love will prevail.

Always remember that everyone has a purpose and until that purpose is found and fulfilled you are not done. I know that life is sometimes unfair and hard but no one ever said it would be easy. There are tons of people in worse shape than you and that many more that need you. Take note that as long as you still have life you have a chance but be aware we are not promised tomorrow so start loving today.

Trust

Do you trust me? That is one of the most famous lines that just about everybody have heard at some point or another. Let's face it trusting someone isn't that easy anymore. Based on what the world has evolved into practically everyone has a huge barrier around the trust factor.

Trustful relations were once something people were eagerly willing to take a chance on developing. Years ago if someone saw or since that you were a worthy person then they would tryingly give you the benefit of doubt to building a loyal reputation. Trust became the foundation of allowing one to establish credibility and self-worthiness. The two strongly committed words are spoken in high volumes like wedding vows.

For the past generations, many people relied on being trusted in order to get through daily life expectancies such as feeding their families. In those days how highly you were thought of gave great precision to the things you could accomplish. Sadly, those times have truly changed. People have gained a lack of care as to what one think of them. Many threw self-worth and trust down the drain by not withholding up to their end of the bargain. As we all see now trust is dispensed only in very small amounts similar to that of a teaspoon. Not only do things now have to be paid for up front but people in general have taken precautions to narrow the stairs that lead to being scammed in any way by dishonesty.

With things being tough and times getting harder backs are turned leaving trust in a solitude state. It no longer comes easy. Earning trust these days have great demands. You have to prove without lingering doubt that you have what it takes to be trusted. As time goes on I can only presume that trusting someone will continue to get harder. The deceit, violence, and criminal nature of people have demolished what use to be an atmosphere partially opened to the belief of good deeds. With so much corruption at large there is no turning back. You cannot point out the good from the bad anymore. So many are disguised with the look and tongue of purity yet contain scandalous itineraries. It's a horrific thing to know that so many distrusts and negative persuasive con-related actions are roaming right outside our doors and possibly in our homes.

The way things have changed. We all are forced into untrustworthy situations. The high value of monetary deficits due to the lack of jobs and political scams at all levels is pushing us all in one corner making us vulnerable to wrongful acts. The ironic thing is that if circumstances don't get better everyone will have to trust someone despite what's at risk and whether they know that person or not.

Trust

There is absolutely nothing wrong with extending or gaining trust. Whichever way is present the key is to be careful. A lot of misleading things and perpetual lies are out there waiting. It is never a good feeling to be devoured by false assumptions. When betrayal of trust arrives, it steals something far more of value than a thief in the night. A thief you don't let in but a person you trust you does. You never see betrayal coming and least expects it at the time and day of its presence. It always leaves you in a state of disbelief and shock. The pain that you sometimes endure from the broken trust can put your heart in a very throbbing, chilling, and stiff place as if it was frost bitten. Even when there may be signs of disloyalty many people fail to recognize them, notice them when it's too late or just over look them altogether.

There is one known fact about trust and its deceptive counterpart. They highly differ when it comes to discrimination. Trust has always picked and choose who, what, when, where, and why. So generally it has a preference. The deception it vigorously carries at different intervals has an open-door policy to all. It is so unlimited to the degree, nature, and existence of everything and everyone. As dramatizing as it may be children even babies are victims robbed of trust before they can speak or spell the word. There is no justification for that. This issue is so deep no ruler can measure its depth. It is colder than Alaska, the Arctic, and way beneath anything a thermostat can read. We will never be able to put our finger on the actual weight of trust. Knowing that the people in this world are so unbalanced we all have to cautiously to the best of our ability think and act precisely. Every devious plan is not targeted toward the next individual. There are more people than you know who don't trust or often deceive themselves. It's a shame that the same trust that holds us together can and has with ease separated us from either ourselves or others.

Trust is one of those things that we have no choice but to juggle. It goes around from hand to hand.

Surely, it provides people with a variation of things ranging from since of security to a lifetime of fear. Facing uncertainty we still try to lean toward one another daily. Yes, somewhere and somehow this cycle is often broken and isn't simple to repair. As human beings it is in our nature to reach out constantly. Therefore, the circulation and revolving doors of trust will never end.

Having fun, cracking jokes, and playing around are cool but something as profound as trust needs to be taken more serious. It is the main ingredient necessary to keep any form of friendship, partnership, and agreement stable and lasting. If you have a collaboration of trust holds on to it.

Trust

Avoid at all cost doing anything to weaken that connection. Given the slightest opportunity to collapse trust will never be the same, especially if it leaves a scar. Trust is really a big commodity. It can help shape your life by adding more dimensions to your character. No, we can’t control how other people manipulate trust, but we can take account for our own actions. Playing with trust will only lead to riffraff and hurtfulness. Remember there is a boomerang effect to all things. Whether it is sooner or later what we do in life will come back to catch up with us. This implies to the works of both good and bad. Having this in mind we shouldn't take trust as a game. It may have times where you will have to roll the dice, take a chance, or pay a fee, but it's more realistic than Monopoly.

You know today we all are being put through trials and tests. As we go through life and face the millions of challenges that sometimes tear us down we lose belief. However, to regain our confidence or the endurance to strive again we must put trust in someone or something. How much trust is always the question that needs to be figured out? No matter what the level of trust it turns out to be we must understand that a little goes a long way.

Basic decisions that are made every day are set to have windows of trust and dishonesty. If it was known which window would be broken than the route to take would be a cinch to choose. Sorry to say but things aren't that straight forward. The choice of which path we want to go down is ours but what lies among that path we have no power to determine. Most of the time we trust our instincts and aren't sure whether they will fail us or not. Even though they have and may let us down again that doesn't stop us from following them. This goes to show that trust is something so naturally embedded in us.

Trusted in are not the only things within our eye sight or reach. We trust a multitude of things not even seen nor felt. Our great father who has given us life is never visible or in arms' length, but we trust in him. The remarkable side to it is that no matter how many times we let him down he still is there trusting and believing in us. There will always be times of disparity and no one person will go about things the same. Rather than closing the doors on one another, we need to relinquish fear and reestablish the opportunity of trust. The rough economy shadowing everyone may have gone bad but it doesn't mean that we have to. Making a difference or setting a trend has to start from somewhere. So trust in yourself to be that person that everyone no longer perceives to exist.

Friendship

As long as life has existed it has never been meant for us to be alone. From the very beginning, we had our creator. Then surrounding us is a world fulfilled with thousands of living things. Things that we sought out to know, learn, and dwell with. As humans we have the tendency to socialize, branch out, and engage ourselves with others. Our act of being social brought forth special relations of communication and sharing. These feeling to converse transformed into what we call today, friendships. Whether people were relatively linked or not friendships arose from everywhere. With its rapid growth and changing sectors it became an accommodation to our way of life.

In the earlier days, it wasn't hard to gain friends. People didn't have the many luxuries of today such as TVs, video games, toys, computers and other broad choices. There was nothing left to do outside of work and chores other than finding someone to play or interact with. So during those times friendship came easy. It was often as pure as filtered water and as simple as drinking it. It didn't consist of purposely devious acts of betrayal that nowadays lurks conscientiously within. One of the things we have previously known to be and thought was so easy to form turned out to be one of the hardest things to accomplish. The spoken notion that true friends are hard to find is short of a myth but every bit of the truth.

When encountering friends there is one critical step that most people fail to evaluate. This huge factor is getting to know ourselves first. How do we expect to acquire the knowledge and friendship of another person without collectively learning or knowing our own self-being? Understanding, evaluating, and becoming familiar with our own friendly tactics within will give us more awareness, insight, and the closest concept to what a friend really means. Leaving such a well needed diagnosis out could already be the ending as well as the beginning of what could have been a beautiful friendship. It's simply like trying to start a car with a dead battery. It's not going to work, even if you get a boost it will only last so long before it dies again.

Be mindful that it's not easy finding your true inner self and character. Many of us are still lost this very day as to who we are and whether we're happy with or like ourselves. Don't worry though because just like most things finding yourself and real friendship comes with time and age. It often takes those short increments of friendships and a few caring friends along the way to help you build, bring out, and discover your hidden soul. Try being your own very best friend first. It's the leading tool to everlasting friendships.

Friendship

In the current market of friendships formed now no one wants to take the leading role to keep such a bond well grounded. So many lose focus and turn their backs relying on the expectations of another person rather than applying themselves unconditionally. This factor alone has contributed to the existence of various types of friendships. Friendships that well too often are formed based upon foolish tendencies and limited agendas.

One of the best ways of being a good friend is to be you. No matter how one tries you can never play dress-up and gain a legendary friendship with an imitation impression of self-actions. It is often too late for restoration when someone finally realizes that the price of a gourmet friendship is well worth it. It's a lifetime healthier compared to one cheaper than the dollar menu and full of fatty fibs. More importantly, the characteristic of the person you choose to befriend or make your best friend shouldn't matter. It could be a parent, sibling, neighbor, dating mate, husband, wife, or any other title of a living being. Things that should be detrimental and important for everyone is the love, care, concern, respect, honesty, closeness, open doors, how you're perceived, and socialization of the friendship. If there is anyone in this world that believes at some point in their life, they don't need a shoulder to lean on other than their own then they are short changing themselves. Having such a diluted thought shall only put them in the position to reap the consequences of an unwise soul destined for loneliness and hardship.

All friendships have unpredictable measures of longevity and stability. With the life span of today being shorter than its historical eras, there is no room for elevated egos. It's time to savor every bundle of hugs, harmony of laughter and reflections of extravagant mementos. As with all ships of any kind, three major possibilities of sailing, sinking, or being anchored can apply. Friendships have been known to sail smoothly far and beyond, be secured and tightly anchored, and deeply sink due to worldly wrath. If there is anything you can do to better or sustain your friendship then take the opportunity to do so. Avoid getting lost along a yellow brick road full of mixed emotions seeking to find another dear and irreplaceable friend.

There are a million reasons and things surrounding us that put us in the vulnerability of needing a friend. It has always been said that it is ok to talk to your own-self but never to answer. Having someone trust worthy in your presence that can give you a response or answer, which you can confide in and share with is more than enough that you can ask for. Nevertheless, be aware of people that you think are your friend. Not everyone has your best interest at heart. There are many imposters posing to be exactly what they are not, your friend. Instead they are really mare associates whom might envy you, be competitive, or just simply misguiding. A true friend is totally the opposite. They will be supportive, helpful, encouraging, and give you good advice. Therefore, take the time to care about yourself by choosing friends who will care too. We all need one or more because life demands it.

Visually noticing, hard economic times have interfered with friends coming together. Finances, stress, depression, and/or other conditions can pull friends apart. What we fail to realize is that these times are the best times to pull together. It's one of the ways to tell who is or isn't a real friend. Besides, getting through these difficulties with each other will only make the friendship stronger. A friend can joyfully uplift your spirit and push you in the right direction to better things and fight back. Watch how the pressures of life diminish when you stir in the ingredients of the spare of the moment fun and laughter. So if you think about it having friends and joining them for various venues is like medicine. Socialization is healing to the soul. No, you can't keep them in your medicine cabinet, but they can be just one phone call away. Plus like many medical dosages, friends come in different amounts and times needed.

Friendship

Looking at the seriously important factors and vaguely just because, consider hurdling up whenever possible. To better the outcome make a theme event out of whatever you all decide to do, take turns hosting, and do it often. There is nothing wrong with a shop-a-thon, game day, cook out, road trip, or simply hanging out.

Not one thing in this world is perfect and that includes friendships. They have both glorious horizons and painful pitfalls. In them, everyone makes mistakes and needs to learn to forgive and forget. You hear a lot of people say the only one they need by their side is the lord. This is not a false statement, but at the same time he put people in your life for a reason.

The friends whom you have once attained and currently have gained all give a descriptive story about your life's travels and leading destination. The ability to acquire friends is a gift given to us all. Be grateful, appreciative, and thankful for all that you come in connection with because every encounter has a purpose. The only person that wants to travel down a lonely road or empty highway is a hitchhiker. One with no clear grounds, common sense of direction, and is acceptable to wherever they end up. You can dodge that path if you imbed it in your heart not to take friendship for granted.

Family

Majority of things in this day in time isn't made as good as they were years ago. Like automobiles, furniture wood, and cotton for pillows, families have changed too. Regardless whether big or small, family structure, morale, and values have been distorted. What the older heads, our grandparents or great grandparents, have fought so hard to build and install in each of us has been forgotten. Without doubt, family in every aspect supposes to be ultimately first, but today it is disgracefully last.

As time has revealed there is no more unity in families. A bond that was once held so tightly together is broken.

The last name who spoke for everybody no longer carries its echo in fine tune. How did something of such value that distinguished us accordingly with great respect depreciate? Do the symbolic labels of being Mr., Mrs., Miss., or Ms. Such and such mean anything anymore? For those of you who know it or not family is extremely important. That union of blood that flows among all of us needs to be unclogged. Having a family our own family expresses a lot about us and plays a significant part in our life's past, present, and future. If we didn't have that family name then we wouldn't know precisely the background as to who we are and where we came from. Now with so much at stake and the aggression of times we need to break the division and reunite.

Many families strive to stay together while others care less about one another. Having all the tough battles of day to day life make it hard for people to build and keep families grounded. With so much at large many choose the easiest route of walking away and becoming distant rather than squaring away their differences and reaching a common respectable state of acquaintance. Pay attention to the fact that some family matters are more or less troublesome. Then sometimes there may be no issues at all. These various periods are called trials. Trials, which not only one family have but all families, including my own.

The testing of times is truly here. Just like anything else family strength and stability are being examined. Now realistically the results of this exam can be good or bad depending upon each family's durability. The down side to it is that family members may become angry, violent, unsociable, separated, less loving and caring, and last but not least never have an existing connection again. A score along this range shows a sign of a family easily able to be erupted. Don't let this be your family. Tend to it the same way you take the necessary steps and precautions to secure your money and other valuables. The upside is that they realize their differences, mistakes, feeling of sorrow and love, ability to apologize and stay connected, and lastly, they're family. This average represents a family of continuous growth and development. Yes, it's true when they say that blood may be thicker than water but the natural strong force of water can sometimes wash blood away. Keep this in mind and aim to sustain a family-like legacy.

There is no such thing as a perfect family. They don't come with manuals but do contain numerous parts. No one family is exactly like another. Being individually packaged they all take time to make, assemble, and keep sturdy. Each has its own hurdles and dilemmas to face and overcome. So very similar to that of an assembly line, families can't be ran without having a defect somewhere down the line.

Love; Trust; Friendship; & Family

It's a struggle to keep families intact but every little effort count. We all know that things in life make it difficult for families to come together. Many people have a rigid work life, extensive schooling, or heavy financial matters that get in the way of family rituals. Important as these things are they should not be excuses for a lack of family time. Remember that while they only last a certain length of hours a day, family is 24 hours every day. Of course, it is good to have dinner at the table together and share interesting conversations but sometimes this is impossible. Instead of leaving a highly essential time out try focusing on any time that is available. It doesn't matter, whether it's during breakfast, taking the kids to school, lunch or brunch, an evening snack, a bedtime story, or just simply passing each other by. It will truly help and make a huge difference. Plus, I know everyone have either had Sunday dinners or at least heard of them. Regardless of all things, hesitate to worry if that particular day isn't doable because any day with family is justifiable for a delicious meal. The key to it all is to be able to talk to and work with one another, be openly, compromise, and initially do what we encourage our kids to do every day, participate.

Has anyone ever taken the time to diagnose and break down what family really means? If not do so because it will show you how vital family is. Try using your own approach and concept as to what your family means to you. I come to find that family has not only one definition but several huge defining statements. First of all, family isn't simple. It is one of the most complex things on earth and in life, but is so vaguely needed. We all know that families have roots. Roots that sprout, perform growth, and are very essential. During every stage and cycle of growth, there is something new developing, which gives families their distinctive traits. So to see or understand family in only one way gives it less meaning and is an understatement. Broaden your views, horizons, aspects, and insight of your family and in family's nature altogether. The ocean is not the only thing that's deep and contains drowning articles. Family has just as much depth and not everything is on the surface. Here are five meaningful layers of family, from the letters exterior to the word's interior. Family means:

- Forever a member in limitless years
- Forgiving all matters, including loveless yesterdays
- Finding amazing moments involving laughter's yodel
- Flourishing against major indifferences leashing you-all
- Fondly admiring memories, including little younglings.

Pondering on the thought, relative, and devotion of family understand that no one human being created on the face of this earth is or has ever been without some kind of family. Letting an irreplaceable thing such as family slip throw the cracks in the ground underneath our feet to be buried so deep in the earth's crust will cause gigantic potholes. Potholes located directly in the heart of our land's surface that make the largest volcano look like a firecracker.

Family is comprised of so much. There are heirlooms, inheritances, and extraordinary historical roots that are sometimes traceable. Family is now! Take advantage of the extended warranty on life, which is continuously given daily. Beware that just like any other warranty it has an expiration date. So get back your family before it's too late.

About the Author

Glanda Woods is a new writer. She is proud to have the privilege to write this book. As she awoke early one morning it was a gift and a calling presented to her. She hopes to reach out to a multitude of people. Her writings are written to send a message and inspire. Her life's story along with other's life stories, numerous blessings, patience, thankfulness, miraculous insight, and many inspirations has helped bring her the ability to understand and document these writings. She is working on another book. She is the mother of two, Kayla and James, living in Michigan.

www.ingramcontent.com/pod-product-compliance
Ingram Content Group UK Ltd.
Pitfield, Milton Keynes, MK11 3LW, UK
UKHW041840200726
13854UKWH00003BA/1231

9 781257 834297